CHRISTMAS REINDEER

Contributing Writer
Carolyn Quattrocki

Illustrations
Susan Spellman

Publications International, Ltd.

It was Christmas Eve in Reindeer Land! All the little reindeer were excited because Santa Claus would visit that night. To pass the time, they went skating and sledding and built snowmen. What fun it was to play in the snow!

Fun for all except one little reindeer named Ruby. The other reindeer wouldn't let her play with them. "Look at funny Ruby!" they cried. "Her nose is redder than a tomato. And look how it shines!"

Ruby tried to cover her nose with some dirt. But nothing could change the fact that Ruby's nose was big and red and very shiny!

That night before bed, Ruby looked outside and saw a great fog that covered all the houses and trees.

"I hope Santa will be able to see through all this fog," said Ruby. "I want to be sure he finds my house." Ruby knew she had been a good reindeer that year.

Up at the North Pole, Santa was getting ready for his big trip. He was worried about the thick fog. "I'll have to fly slowly so I won't bump into anything," he thought.

Santa hitched his reindeer to his sleigh, and off they flew. At first the street lamps and house lights kept the sleigh on course. At each house Santa worked quickly, being sure to leave the right presents for each little girl and boy.

Santa arrived at Ruby's house at midnight, and it was very dark. The fog made the night so dark that Santa couldn't see well. He ran right into a chair trying to find his way around! Things were taking much longer than Santa thought they would. He was worried that he wouldn't be able to make it to all the houses before morning!

Then Santa noticed a red glow that was coming from beneath a door.

Carefully and quietly, Santa opened the door to Ruby's bedroom. He was surprised that the room was not dark. There was a glowing red light all around.

While Ruby slept, her shiny red nose lighted the room so well that Santa could see into every corner.

Santa thought Ruby was the most amazing reindeer he had ever seen. Then he had a great idea! He leaned over and woke up Ruby.

Santa explained that the fog was slowing him down, so he might not get to every house before morning."

"Do you really think I can help?" asked Ruby.

Santa answered, "Oh yes! You can guide the sleigh through the fog. Your shiny red nose will lead the way!"

Ruby was very excited. Before leaving, she wrote a note to her family. It said, "I've gone to help out Santa. I'll be back by morning."

Ruby pranced from the house with her red nose glowing. Santa's other reindeer could not believe their eyes. They had never seen a reindeer with such a shiny red nose.

Santa hitched Ruby to his team, and up they flew. Even with the fog, they could now fly very quickly. Ruby's nose made the whole sky bright. Their work went so fast that Santa finished filling the last stocking just as the sun was peeping over the hills.

The morning sun woke Ruby's parents, and they found the note that Ruby left in the night. They were very proud of her. Everyone knows that riding with Santa is the best honor a reindeer can have.

"Our Ruby has gone to help Santa!" shouted Ruby's mom and dad. All the reindeer in Reindeer Land gathered by Ruby's house to wait for her return. Some did not believe that quiet little Ruby could be the hero of Christmas!

Soon Santa's sleigh came into sight, and Ruby was leading the way. What a great cheer there was!

When the sleigh pulled to a stop, Santa said, "Ruby, I've never had a reindeer as brave as you. I would have been lost without you."

Then the crowd shouted, "Hurray for Ruby!" But Ruby was a bashful hero. When the crowd cheered, Ruby blushed, and her nose was redder than ever.